A Garth Williams Treasury of Best-Loved Golden Books

A Garth Williams Treasury of Best-Loved Golden Books

with an introduction by
Leonard S. Marcus

 A Golden Book · New York

Golden Books Publishing Company, Inc., New York, New York 10106

Library of Congress Cataloging-in-Publication Data

A Garth Williams treasury of best loved Golden Books / with an introduction by Leonard S. Marcus ; illustrations by Garth Williams.

p. cm.

Contents: A tale of tails / Elizabeth H. MacPherson.—Baby farm animals / Garth Williams.— Three bedtime stories / Garth Williams.—Animal friends / Jane Werner.— The Golden sleepy book / Margaret Wise Brown.—The friendly book / Margaret Wise Brown.— Home for a bunny / Margaret Wise Brown.—The sailor dog / Margaret Wise Brown.— The kitten who thought he was a mouse / Miriam Norton.—Mister dog / Margaret Wise Brown.

ISBN 0-307-10889-9

1. Children's stories, American. [1. Short stories.] I. Williams, Garth, ill. II. Marcus, Leonard S., date.

PZ5. G3155 2001   [E]—dc21   00-046258

❧ Contents ❧

Garth Williams, circa 1955

Introduction

The droll, full-hearted, masterful art of Garth Williams (1912–1996) reveals a world of wonders in which childhood, and the things children love, take center stage. In a richly productive career spanning more than forty years, Williams illustrated an extraordinary list of children's classics, including E. B. White's *Stuart Little* (1945) and *Charlotte's Web* (1952), Laura Ingalls Wilder's Little House books (1953), Margery Sharp's *The Rescuers* (1959), and Jack Prelutsky's *Ride a Purple Pelican* (1986). In 1948, he became one of the brightest stars of the Golden Books imprint, a groundbreaking publishing experiment for which he produced much of his most vibrant full-color art. Ten of Williams's memorable books for the Golden list have been gathered together in this treasure-laden treasury—in several instances with art and text restored to their uncut, original form for the first time in more than a generation.

Founded in 1942 as a joint venture of Simon & Schuster and the Western Printing Company, Golden Books became *the* children's publishing phenomenon of the postwar baby boom years. At a time when few bookshops stocked children's literature and when the average picture book sold for $1.75, millions of parents reached for the brightly illustrated 25-cent Little Golden volumes, which they found at local five-and-dimes and supermarkets. These appealing books (and their larger, also modestly priced "Big Golden" counterparts) were not only a bargain; they were *very* good. As a Golden artist, Williams teamed up with some of the finest children's book writers of his generation.

Williams was an elegantly sporty, mercurial man who often worked on several books at a time, each in a different room of whatever house he was living in at the moment. He was the American picture book's Fred Astaire: outwardly blithe, but a private perfectionist who sketched a subject until it had become second nature. Armed with empathy, dazzling technical skills, and a deep feeling for nature, Williams created virtuoso children's book art that celebrates home life and seasonal change while offering young readers a garden glimpse of a wider, wilder world of adventure. Revered by his contemporaries as an illustrator's illustrator, he set a high standard that continues to inspire artists today. Yet Williams himself never won the Caldecott Medal, nor received any other major formal recognition for his illustration work.

Garth Williams was born on April 16, 1912, in New York City, to British parents. His father, Hamilton Williams, drew cartoons for leading humor magazines on both sides of the Atlantic, including *Punch* and *Judge.* His mother, Fiona, painted landscapes. "Everybody in my home was always either painting or drawing," Williams once recalled. He never questioned whether to become an artist himself, only what kind and on what terms.

After a seminomadic childhood spent in rural New Jersey, Canada, and France, he moved with his family to England. Anxious for a career that combined creative satisfaction with the promise of a solid income, Williams studied architecture. But with the coming of the Great Depression, demand for architects' services fell off sharply, and Williams, with his characteristically devil-may-care brand of pragmatism, concluded that he might as well try his luck at fine art instead. In 1936, he won the British Prix de Rome for sculpture, an honor that netted him two years of study in Italy.

Once back in England, however, the restless Williams struck out in yet another direction, taking a job with a magazine publisher. Then, with the outbreak of World War II, he joined the British Red Cross Civil Defense in London. In 1941, after suffering injuries of his own during the Blitz, Williams returned to New York City, where he freelanced for *The New Yorker* and other magazines before illustrating E. B. White's *Stuart Little.* The experience set him on his future course as a children's book artist. Soon afterward, he met

Margaret Wise Brown, a gifted writer who shared his artistic verve and spirit of enterprise. They became friends and in 1948, Brown and Williams debuted on the Golden list as the author and illustrator of *The Golden Sleepy Book.*

Believing it the illustrator's job to tailor his work to the text at hand, Williams trained himself to draw and paint in a variety of styles, ranging from the lapidary precision of the watercolors for his own *Baby Farm Animals* (1953); to the more broadly comic paintings for Miriam Norton's *The Kitten Who Thought He Was a Mouse* (1954); to the unbuttoned, cartoonlike pen-and-ink and watercolor illustrations for Brown's *The Sailor Dog* (1953).

In all its variations, Williams's art displays a canny knack for projecting human qualities and expressions onto a story's furry and feathery players. Starting from a close knowledge of nature, Williams reveled in the magic and mischief of "redesigning" his subjects just enough to achieve the desired illusion. Williams's creatures have the *furriest* fur and *featheriest* feathers. At the same time, they live out core emotions—the love of a parent and child for each other, the heady excitement of making a new friend, the supreme comfort of safely settling into one's own bed—that we easily recognize as our own.

Williams's joyful art is above all a triumph of honest emotion over pat sentiment. No illustrator of his generation caught more accurately the subtle mix of intense curiosity, fierce optimism, and fledgling fear that all children balance and bear as they take their first steps out into the world. In Williams's illustrations, endearing bunnies, kittens, puppies, and the occasional boy and girl meet one another—and the little surprises life puts in their paths—with natural grace, unfussy dignity, and open eyes. Brave hearts all, they embrace the world in its bigness and mystery, and in doing so have the time of their lives.

The spirited art of Garth Williams invites us to do the same.

—*Leonard S. Marcus*

A Tale of Tails

written by Elizabeth H. MacPherson

My dog has a tail he can wag when he's glad.

My cat has a tail she can swish when she's mad.

A very fine tail
has the big kangaroo,

And so has the lion
that lives in the zoo.

The horse has a tail for brushing off flies.

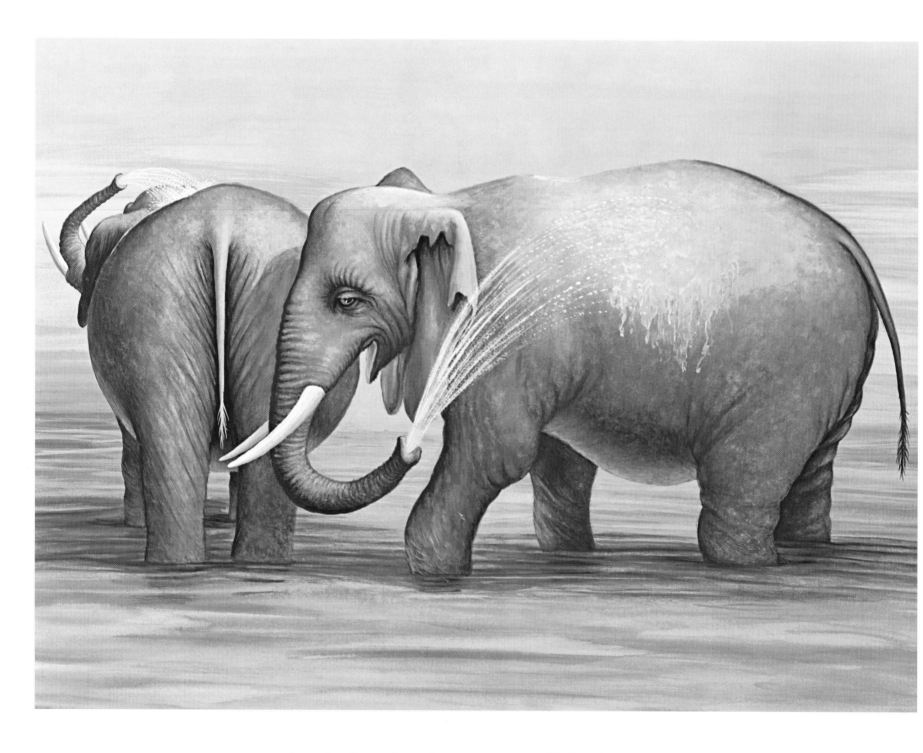

An elephant's tail is quite small for his size.

A monkey can swing
by his tail from a tree.

Oh, everyone has a tail
except me.

A fish has a tail
that can help him to swim.

A mouse has a tail
that is longer than him.

The tail of the rabbit
is fluffy and small.

The tail of the whale
is the largest of all.

The pig has a tail with a curl and a bend.

A snake is all tail with a head on one end.

A polliwog's tail disappears as he grows.

And even a snail has a tail, I suppose.

The little gray squirrels that live in our tree
Have tails that are bushy as bushy can be.

And such a small tail
has the big polar bear,
I doubt very much
that he knows it is there.

A bird has a tail that can
help him to fly.

If they all have tails, then why haven't I?

Baby Farm Animals

written by Garth Williams

Baby Cats are called kittens. They love to play on the farm. At night the farmer gives them fresh cow's milk and they curl up together in the big red barn.

Baby Rabbit lives in a hutch, which is her tiny little house. She sniffs noses with the kittens and puppies because they are all friends.

Baby Guinea Pigs also have a hutch. Have you ever seen a guinea pig's tail?

"That rabbit has been up to some mischief," says the brown guinea pig.

Baby Donkey loves to eat juicy carrots. He is sitting down because he is tired. Somebody is trying to make him walk with those carrots tied on the end of a stick.

"I know that trick," he says.

Baby Ducklings swim in the pond with their wide, webbed feet.

"Why don't you come for a swim?" they ask the chicks.

Baby Chicks cannot swim.

"Mother says we must look for worms and stay out of the water," they reply.

Baby Pigs are called piglets. They love
to sleep on clean straw. A piglet digs with his
nose, which is called a snout. If you pick him
up or chase him, he will squeal for his
mother—*Oink, oink, oink.*

Baby Cow is called a calf. She has soft-brown eyes and says *Moooo,* which usually means she wants her mother and some milk. When she was only a few hours old, she could go for a walk with her mother and eat grass, daisies, and dandelions. Her father is a big fierce bull.

Baby Puppies stay in the stable, close to the horses. They growl and bark at strangers. They pretend that this shoe is a big bad wolf. They growl and bark at it, too.

Baby Goats are called kids, just like little boys and girls. They try to knock each other down by butting their heads together. Their father has horns and a pointed beard.

Baby Swans are called cygnets. Now they are covered with smoke-colored down. Soon they will have pure white feathers and long, long necks.

Baby Gosling will be a big gray goose some day. See her brother with his head under the water? He is looking for something to eat.

Baby Horse is called a foal. She could walk the same day she was born. Now, after a week, she gallops. When she is two years old, she will be a beautiful horse, and people will be able to ride on her back. Perhaps she will win a race.

Baby Sheep is called a lamb. She is crying for her mother— *Baa, baa, baa!* If she looks in the barn, she will find her.

In the spring, the farmer will shear the lamb's wool.

Baby Pony is taking Kitten and Puppy for a ride.
He is a Shetland pony, so he will not grow much bigger.

How many baby farm
animals can you name?

Three Bedtime Stories

The Three Little Kittens • The Three Little Pigs • The Three Bears

retold by *Garth Williams*

❧ The Three Little Kittens ❧

The three little kittens,
They lost their mittens,
And they began to cry,
"Oh Mother dear,
We sadly fear
Our mittens we have lost!"

"What! Lost your mittens,
You naughty kittens?
Then you shall have no pie."
"Meow, meow, meow!"

The three little kittens,
They found their mittens,
And they began to cry,
"Oh Mother dear,
See here, see here,
Our mittens we have found!"

"What! Found your mittens,
You good little kittens?
Then you shall have some pie."
"Purr, purr, purr."
The three little kittens
Put on their mittens,
And soon ate up the pie.

"Oh Mother dear,
We greatly fear
Our mittens we have soiled!"
"What! Soiled your mittens,
You naughty kittens?"
Then they began to sigh,
"Meow, meow, meow!"

The three little kittens,
They washed their mittens,
And hung them up to dry.
"Oh Mother dear,
Look here, look here,
Our mittens we have washed!"

"What! Washed your mittens?
You darling kittens!
But I smell a rat close by!
Hush, hush, hush!"

The Three Little Pigs

Once upon a time three little pigs went out into the world to seek their fortunes.

The first thing each of them had to do was build a house to live in.

The first little pig met a man carrying a bundle of straw.

"Please, sir," he said, "give me some straw to build myself a house."

The straw house was quickly built, and the little pig was just settling down nicely when a big bad wolf knocked at the door and said:

"Little pig, little pig, let me come in!"

"Not by the hair on my chinny chin chin!" said the first little pig.

Then the big bad wolf huffed and he puffed, and he blew the house in.

He ate up the fat little pig. And that was the end of the first little pig.

The second little pig built himself a house of sticks. He was just putting the finishing touches on the window curtains when the big bad wolf knocked at the door and said:

"Little pig, little pig, let me come in!"

"Not by the hair on my chinny chin chin!" said the second little pig.

Then the big bad wolf huffed and he puffed, and he puffed and he huffed, and he blew the house in.

He ate up the second little pig. And that was the end of *that* little pig.

Now the third little pig had built himself a house of bricks. It took him much longer to build than a straw house, or a house of sticks.

The little pig had just put the last brick in place when the big bad wolf knocked at the door and said:

"Little pig, little pig, let me come in!"

"Not by the hair on my chinny chin chin!" said the third little pig.

Then the big bad wolf huffed and he puffed, and he puffed and he huffed. But he could not blow the house in!

The brick house stayed there, with the fat little pig safe inside it.

"It's no good hiding, little pig," said the wolf. "I shall come down the chimney."

"Come right ahead!" said the little pig. And he put a big pot of water on the fire to boil.

The big bad wolf came down the chimney and landed right in the pot of boiling water.

That night, the third little pig had wolf stew for dinner. And *that* was the end of the big bad wolf.

❧ The Three Bears ❧

Once upon a time there were three bears—a great big father bear, a middle-sized mother bear, and a little baby bear.

They lived in a cozy house in the forest. And every morning before breakfast, the three bears went for a walk while their porridge cooled.

One day a little girl, who was called Goldilocks because of her golden curls, went for a walk in the forest.

Presently, she came to the house of the three bears.

Knock knock knock at the door went Goldilocks. But of course there was no answer. For the three bears were out on their walk.

So Goldilocks went into the house.

She saw three chairs. She sat in Father Bear's great big chair. It was much too hard.

She sat in Mother Bear's middle-sized chair. It was much too soft.

She sat in Baby Bear's little chair. It was just right! But the little chair broke all to pieces.

"How hungry I am!" said Goldilocks when she saw the three bowls of porridge.

She tasted the porridge in Father Bear's great big bowl. It was much too hot.

She tasted the porridge in Mother Bear's middle-sized bowl. It was much too cold.

She tasted the porridge in Baby Bear's little bowl. It was just right! And Goldilocks ate it all up.

Then up the stairs went Goldilocks to take a nap.

She tried Father Bear's great big bed. It was much too hard.

She tried Mother Bear's middle-sized bed. It was much too soft.

She tried Baby Bear's little bed. It was just right! Goldilocks lay down on it and fell fast asleep.

Soon, the three bears came home.

"Someone has been sitting in my chair!" said Father Bear in a great big voice.

"And someone has been sitting in my chair!" said Mother Bear in a middle-sized voice.

"Someone has been sitting in my chair!" said Baby Bear in a little baby voice. "And now my chair is broken!"

"Someone has been tasting my porridge!" said Father Bear in a great big voice.

"And someone has been tasting my porridge!" said Mother Bear in a middle-sized voice.

"Someone has been tasting my porridge!" said Baby Bear in a little baby voice. "And someone has eaten it all up!"

Then up the stairs they went.

"Someone has been lying in my bed!" said Father Bear in a great big voice.

"And someone has been lying in my bed!" said Mother Bear in a middle-sized voice.

"Someone has been lying in my bed!" said Baby Bear in a little baby voice. "And someone is still there!"

Then Goldilocks woke up and saw the three bears. She got such a fright that she jumped right up and ran down the stairs, out of the house, and into the forest.

And the three bears never saw Goldilocks again.

❧ Animal Friends ❧

written by Jane Werner

Once upon a time, in a small house deep in the woods, lived a lively family of animals.

There was Miss Kitty, Mr. Pup, Brown Bunny, Little Chick, Fluffy Squirrel, Poky Turtle, and Tweeter Bird.

Each had a little chest, and a little bed and chair, and they took turns cooking on their little kitchen stove.

They got along nicely when it came to sharing toys, being quiet at nap times, and keeping the house neat. But they could not agree on food.

When Miss Kitty cooked, they had milk and catnip tea and little bits of liver on their plates.

Mr. Pup didn't mind the liver, but the other animals were unhappy.

They didn't like any better the bones Pup served them in his turn. Or Bunny's carrot dinners, or Tweeter's tasty worms, or Turtle's ants' eggs, or Squirrel's nuts.

When Bunny fixed the meals, she arranged lettuce leaves and carrot nibbles with artistic taste, but only Tweeter Bird would eat any of them. And when Tweeter served worms and crisp, chewy seeds, only Little Chick would eat them.

But Little Chick liked bugs and beetles even better. Poky Turtle would nibble at them, but what he really hungered for were tasty ants' eggs.

Fluffy Squirrel wanted nuts and nuts and nuts. Without his sharp teeth and his firm paws, the others could not get a nibble from a nut, so they all went hungry when Fluffy fixed the meals.

Finally they all knew that something must be done. They gathered around the fire one cool and cozy evening and talked things over.

"The home for me," said Mr. Pup, "is a place where I can have bones and meat every day."

"I want milk and liver instead of bugs and seeds," said Miss Kitty.

"Nuts for me," said Squirrel.

"Ants' eggs," yawned Turtle.

"Crispy lettuce," whispered Bunny.

"A stalk of seeds," dreamed Bird, "and some worms make a home for me."

"New homes are what we need," said Mr. Pup. And everyone agreed. So next morning they packed their little satchels and said their fond good-byes.

Squirrel waved good-bye to them all. He had decided to stay in the house in the woods.

He started right in gathering nuts. Soon there were nuts in the kitchen stove, nuts in the cupboards, and nuts piled up in all the empty beds. There was scarcely room for that happy little squirrel!

The others walked along until they came to a garden with rows and rows of tasty growing things.

"Here's the home for me," said bright-eyed Brown Bunny, and she settled down there at the roots of a big tree.

Little Chick found a chicken yard full of lovely, scratchy gravel where all kinds of crispy, crunchy bugs lived.

"Here I stay," chirped Chick, squeezing under the fence to join the other chickens there.

Poky Turtle found a pond with a lovely log for napping, half in the sun, half in the shade. Close by the log was a busy, bustling anthill, full of the eggs Turtle loved.

Tweeter Bird found a nest in a tree above the pond, where he could see the world, the seeds on the grasses, and the worms on the ground.

"This is the home for me," sang Bird happily.

Miss Kitty went on until she came to a house where a little girl welcomed her.

"Here is a bowl of milk for you, Miss Kitty," said the little girl, "and a ball of yarn to play with."

So, with a purr, Miss Kitty settled down in her new home.

Mr. Pup found a boy in the house next door. The boy had a bone and some meat for Pup, a bed for him to sleep in, and a handsome collar for him to wear.

"Bow wow," barked Pup. "This is the home for me."

That night, as the animal friends went to sleep, each one said, "At last I've found the best home of all, the very best home for me."

selections from

The Golden Sleepy Book

The Whispering Rabbit · Close Your Eyes · Going to Sleep

written by *Margaret Wise Brown*

🍂 The Whispering Rabbit 🍂

Once there was a sleepy little rabbit
  Who began to yawn—
  And he yawned and he yawned and he yawned
and he yawned,
  "Hmmm————"

He opened his little rabbit mouth when he yawned till you could see his white front teeth and his little round pink mouth, and he yawned and he yawned until suddenly a bee flew into his mouth and he swallowed the bee.

"*Hooo—hooo—,*" said a fat old owl. "Always keep your paw in front of your mouth when you yawn," hooted the owl.

"Rabbits never do that," said the sleepy little rabbit.

"Silly rabbits!" said the owl, and he flew away.

The little rabbit was just calling after him, but when the little rabbit opened his mouth to speak, the bumble-bee had curled up to sleep in his throat—AND—all he could do was whisper.

"What shall I do?" he whispered to a squirrel who wasn't sleepy.

"Wake him up," said the squirrel. "Wake up the bumblebee."

"How?" whispered the rabbit. "All I can do is whisper and I'm sleepy and I want to go to sleep and who can sleep with a bumblebee—"

Suddenly a wise old groundhog popped up out of the ground.

"All I can do is whisper," said the little rabbit.

"All the better," said the groundhog.

"Come here, little rabbit," he said, "and I will whisper to you how to wake up a bumblebee:

"You have to make the littlest noise that you can possibly make because a bumblebee doesn't bother about big noises. He is a very little bee and he is only interested in little noises."

"Like a loud whisper?" asked the rabbit.

"Too loud," said the groundhog, and popped back into his hole.

"A little noise," whispered the rabbit, and he started making little rabbit noises—he made a noise as quiet as the sound of a bird's wing cutting the air, but the bee didn't wake up.

So the little rabbit made the sound of snow falling, but the bee didn't wake up.

So the little rabbit made the sound of a bug breathing and a fly sneezing and grass rustling and a fireman thinking. Still the bee didn't wake up. So the rabbit sat and thought of all the little sounds he could think of— What could they be?

A sound quiet as snow melting, quiet as a flower growing, quiet as an egg, quiet as— And suddenly he knew the little noise that he would make—and he made it.

It was like a little click made hundreds of miles away by a bumblebee in an apple tree in full bloom on a mountaintop. It was the very small click of a bee swallowing some honey from an apple blossom.

And at that the bee woke up.
He thought he was missing
something, and away he flew.
And then what did the little
rabbit do? That sleepy, sleepy
little rabbit?

He closed his mouth
He closed his eyes
He closed his ears
And he tucked in his paws
And twitched his nose
And he fell sound asleep!

Close Your Eyes

Little donkey on the hill
Standing there so very still
Making faces at the skies
Little donkey, close your eyes.

Silly sheep that slowly crop
Night has come and you must stop
Chewing grass beneath the skies
Silly sheep, now close your eyes.

Little monkey in a tree
Swinging there so merrily
Throwing coconuts at the skies
Little monkey, close your eyes.

Little birds that sweetly sing
Curve your heads beneath your wing
No more whistling in the skies
Little birds, now close your eyes.

Little horses in your stall
Stop your stomping, stop it all
Tails stop switching after flies
Little horses, close your eyes.

Little pigs that snuff about
No more snorting with your snout
No more squealing to the skies
Noisy pigs, now close your eyes.

Old black cat down in the barn
Keeping four black kittens warm
Winds are quiet in the skies
Dear old black cat, close your eyes.

Little child all tucked in bed
Looking like a sleepyhead
Stars are quiet in the skies
Little child, now close your eyes.

Little donkey, close your eyes.

Silly sheep, now close your eyes.

Little monkey, close your eyes.

Little birds, now close your eyes.

Little horses, close your eyes.

Noisy pigs, now close your eyes.

Dear old black cat, close your eyes.

Little child, now close your eyes.

✿ Going to Sleep ✿

All over the world the animals are going to sleep—the birds and the bees, the horse, the butterfly, and the cat.

In their high nests by the ocean the fish hawks are going to sleep. And how does a young fish hawk go to sleep? The same as any other bird in the world.

She folds her wings and pushes herself deep in the nest, looks around and blinks her eyes three times, takes one long last look over the ocean, then tucks her head under her wing and sleeps like a bird.

And the fish in the sea sleep in the darkened sea when the long green light of the sun is gone. And they sleep like fish, with their eyes wide open in some quiet current of the sea.

And above and beyond under the stars on the land, all the little horses are going to sleep. Some stand up in the still, dark fields and some fold their legs under them and lie down. But they all go to sleep like horses.

Even the bees and the butterflies sleep when the moths begin to fly. And they sleep like bees and butterflies, under a leaf or a stick or a stone, with folded wings and their eyes wide open. For fish and bees and butterflies and flies never close their shiny eyes.

And the old fat bear in the deep dark woods goes into his warm cave to sleep for the whole winter.

So do the groundhogs and the hedgehogs, the skunks and the black-eyed raccoons.

They eat and eat, then sleep until spring—a long warm sleep.

The Friendly Book

written by Margaret Wise Brown

I LIKE CARS

Red cars, Green cars
Sport limousine cars
I like cars

A car in a garage
A car with a load
A car with a flat tire
A car on the road
I like cars.

I LIKE TRAINS

Express trains

Toy trains

Streamline trains

Freight trains

Old trains

Milk trains

Any kind of train
A train in the station
Trains crossing the plains
Trains in a snowstorm
Trains in the rain
I like trains.

I LIKE STARS

Yellow stars
Green stars
Red stars
Blue stars
I like stars
Far stars
Quiet stars
Bright stars
Light stars
I like stars
A star that is shooting
   across the dark sky
A star that is shining
   right straight in your eye
I like stars.

I LIKE SNOW

Cold snow

Slow snow

White snow

Icy snow

I like snow

Snow falling softly with everything still

White in the blue night, white on the sill

White on the trees on the far distant hill

With everything still

I like snow.

I LIKE SEEDS

Mustard seeds, Radish seeds
Corn seeds, Flower seeds
Any kind of seed
Seeds that are sprouting green from the ground
And seeds of the milkweed flying around
I like seeds.

I LIKE BUGS

Black bugs, Green bugs

Bad bugs, Mean bugs

Any kind of bug

A bug in a rug

A bug in the grass

A bug on the sidewalk

A bug in a glass

I like bugs

Round bugs, Shiny bugs

Fat bugs, Buggy bugs

Big bugs, Lady bugs

I like bugs.

I LIKE FISH

Silver fish, Gold fish,

Black fish, Old fish

Young fish, Fishy fish

Any kind of fish

A fish in a pond

A fish in a stream

A fish in the ocean

A fish in a dream

I like fish.

I LIKE DOGS

Big dogs, Little dogs
Fat dogs, Doggy dogs
Old dogs, Puppy dogs
I like dogs
A dog that is barking over the hill
A dog that is dreaming very still
A dog that is running wherever he will
I like dogs.

I LIKE BOATS

Any kind of boat

Tug boats, Tow boats

Large boats, Barge boats

Sail boats, Whale boats

Thin boats, Skin boats

Rubber boats, River boats

Flat boats, Cat boats

U-boats, New boats

Tooting boats, Hooting boats

South American fruit boats

Bum boats, Gun boats

Slow boats, Row boats

I like boats.

I LIKE WHISTLES
Wild whistles, Bird whistles
Far-off heard whistles
Boat whistles, Train whistles
I like whistles
The postman's whistle
The policeman's whistle
The wind that blows away the thistle
Light as the little birds whistle and sing
And the little boy whistling in the spring
The wind that whistles through the trees
And blows the boats across the seas
I like whistles.

I LIKE PEOPLE
Glad people
Sad people
Slow people
Mad people
Big people
Little people
I like people.

Home for a Bunny

written by Margaret Wise Brown

"Spring, spring, spring!" sang the frog.
"Spring!" said the groundhog.

"Spring, spring, spring!" sang the robin.

It was spring.

The leaves burst out.

The flowers burst out.

And robins burst out of their eggs.

It was spring.

In the spring a bunny came down the road.
He was going to find a home of his own.
A home for a bunny,
A home of his own,
Under a rock,
Under a stone,
Under a log,
Or under the ground.
Where would a bunny find a home?

"Where is your home?" he asked the robin.
"Here, here, here," sang the robin. "Here in
this nest is my home."

"Here, here, here," sang the little robins who were about to fall out of the nest. "Here is our home."

"Not for me," said the bunny. "I would fall out of a nest. I would fall on the ground."

So he went on looking for a home.

"Where is your home?" he asked the frog.

"Wog, wog, wog," sang the frog.

"Wog, wog, wog,

Under the water,

Down in the bog."

"Not for me," said the bunny.

"Under the water, I would drown in a bog."

So he went on looking for a home.
"Where do you live?" he asked the groundhog.
"In a log," said the groundhog.

"Can I come in?" said the bunny.
"No, you can't come in my log," said the groundhog.

So the bunny went down the road.
Down the road and down the road he went.
He was going to find a home of his own.

A home for a bunny,
A home of his own,
Under a rock
Or a log
Or a stone.
Where would a bunny
find a home?

Down the road
and down the road
and down the road
he went, until—

He met another bunny.
"Where is your home?"
he asked the bunny.

"Here," said the bunny.
"Here is my home.
Under this rock,
Under this stone,
Down under the ground,
Here is my home."

"Can I come in?" said the bunny.

"Yes," said the other bunny.

And so he did.

And that was his home.

The Sailor Dog

written by Margaret Wise Brown

Born at sea in the teeth of a gale, the sailor was a dog.
Scuppers was his name.

After that he lived on a farm. But Scuppers, born at sea, was a sailor. And when he grew up he wanted to go to sea.

So he went to look for something to go in.

He found a big airplane. "All aboard!" they called. It was going up in the sky. But Scuppers did not want to go up in the sky.

He found a little submarine.
"All aboard!" they called. It was going down
under the sea. But Scuppers did not want to go down under
the sea.

He found a little car. "All aboard!" they called. It was going
over the land. But Scuppers did not want to go over the land.

He found a subway train. "All aboard!" they called. It was
going under the ground. But Scuppers did not want to go
under the ground.

Scuppers was a sailor. He wanted to go to sea.

So Scuppers went over the hills and far away until he came to the ocean. And on the ocean was a ship. It was blowing all its whistles.

"All aboard!" they called.

"All ashore that are going ashore!"

"All aboard!"

So Scuppers went to sea.

The ship began to move slowly along. The wind blew it.

In his ship Scuppers had a little room. In his room he had a hook for his hat, and a hook for his rope, and a hook for his pants, and a hook for his coat, and a hook for his spyglass, and a place for his shoes, and a bunk for a bed to put himself in.

At night Scuppers threw the anchor into the sea and went down to his little room.

He hung his hat on the hook for his hat, and his rope on the hook for his rope, and his pants on the hook for his pants, and his coat on the hook for his coat, and his spyglass on the hook for his spyglass, and he put his shoes under the bed, and got into his bed, which was a bunk, and went to sleep.

Next morning he was shipwrecked.

Too big a storm blew out of the sky. The anchor dragged, and the ship crashed onto the rocks. There was a big hole in it.

Scuppers himself was washed overboard and hurled by huge waves onto the shore.

It was foggy and rainy. There were no houses, and Scuppers needed a house.

But on the beach was lots and lots of driftwood, and an old rusty box stuck in the sand.

Maybe it was a treasure!

It *was* a treasure—to Scuppers.

It was an old-fashioned toolbox with a hammer and nails and an ax and a saw. Everything he needed to build himself a house. So Scuppers started to build a house, all by himself, out of driftwood.

He built a door and a window and a roof and a porch and a floor and some walls, all out of driftwood.

And he found some red bricks and built a big red chimney. And then he lit a fire, and the smoke went up the chimney.

After building his house he was hungry. So he went fishing. He went fishing in a big river. The first fish he caught never came up. The second fish he caught got away. The third fish he caught was too little. But the next fish he caught was—just right.

That night he cooked the fish he caught, and the smoke went up the chimney.

Then the stars came out, and Scuppers was sleepy. So he made a bed of pine branches.

He jumped into his deep green bed and went to sleep. And as he slept he dreamed—

If he could build a house,
he could mend the hole in the ship.

So the next day at low tide he took his toolbox and waded out and hammered planks across the hole in his ship.

At last the ship was fixed.

So he sailed away until he came to a seaport in a foreign land.

By now his clothes were all worn and ripped and blown to pieces. His shirt was torn, his hat and coat were gone, and his shoes were all worn out. Only his pants were still good.

So Scuppers went ashore to buy some clothes at the Army and Navy Store.

First he bought a coat. He found a red one too small. He found a blue one just right. It had brass buttons.

Then he bought a hat. He found a purple one too silly. He found a white one just right.

He needed new shoes. He found some yellow ones too small and some red ones too fancy. Then he found some white ones just right.

Here he is wearing his new hat and his new shoes and his new coat with the shiny brass buttons. (He has a can of polish and a cloth to keep them shiny.)

And he has a new rope and a bushel of fresh oranges.

Now Scuppers wants to go back to his ship. So he goes there.

And at night when the stars come out, he takes one last look through his spyglass. And goes down below to his little room.

He hangs his new hat on the hook for his hat, and he hangs his spyglass on the hook for his spyglass, and he hangs his new coat on the hook for his coat, and his pants on the hook for his pants, and his new rope on the hook for his rope, and his new shoes he puts under his bunk, and himself he puts in his bunk.

And here he is where he wants to be—

A sailor sailing the deep green sea.

HIS SONG

I am Scuppers The Sailor Dog—
I'm Scuppers The Sailor Dog—
I can sail in a gale
Right over a whale
Under full sail
In a fog.

I am Scuppers The Sailor Dog—
I'm Scuppers The Sailor Dog—
With a shake and a snort
I can sail into port
Under full sail
In a fog.

The Kitten Who Thought He Was a Mouse

written by Miriam Norton

There were five Miggses:
Mother and Father Miggs and
Lester and two sisters.

They had, as field mice usually
do, an outdoor nest for summer
in an empty lot, and an indoor
nest for winter in a nearby house.

They were very surprised, one summer day, to find a strange bundle in their nest—a small gray-and-black bundle of fur and ears and legs, with eyes not yet open. They knew by its mewing that the bundle must be a kitten, a lost kitten with no family and no name.

"Poor kitty," said the sisters.
"Let him stay with us," said Lester.
"But a *cat!*" said Mother Miggs.

"Why not?" said Father Miggs.

"We can bring him up to be a good mouse. He need never find out that he is really a cat. You'll see—he'll be a good thing for this family."

"Let's call him Mickey," said Lester.

And that's how Mickey Miggs found his new family and a name.

After his eyes opened, Mickey began to grow up just as mice do, eating all kinds of seeds and bugs, drinking from puddles, and sleeping in a cozy pile of brother and sister mice.

Father Miggs showed him his first tomcat—at a safe distance—and warned him to "keep away from all cats and dogs and people."

Mickey saw his first mousetrap—"The most dangerous thing of all," said Mother Miggs—when they moved to the indoor nest that fall.

He was too clumsy to steal bait from traps himself, so Lester and the sisters had to share with him what they stole.

But Mickey was useful in fooling the household cat, Hazel. He practiced up on meowing—for usually, of course, he squeaked—and became clever at what he thought was *imitating* a cat.

He would hide in a dark corner and then, *"Meow! Meow!"* he'd cry. Hazel would poke around, leaving the pantry shelves unguarded while she looked for the other cat. That gave Lester and his sisters a chance to make a raid on the leftovers.

Poor Hazel! She knew she heard, even smelled, another cat, and sometimes she saw cat's eyes shining in a corner. But no cat ever came out to meet her.

How could she know that Mickey didn't know he was a cat at all, and that he feared Hazel as much as the mousiest mouse would!

And so Mickey Miggs grew, becoming a better mouse all the time and enjoying his life. He loved cheese, bacon, and cake crumbs.

He got especially good at smelling out potato skins, and led the sisters and Lester straight to them every time.

"A wholesome and uncatlike food," said Mother Miggs to Father Miggs approvingly. "Mickey is doing well."

And Father Miggs said to Mother Miggs, "I told you so!"

Then one day, coming from a nap in the wastepaper basket, Mickey met the children of the house, Peggy and Paul.

"Ee-eeeeeek!" Mickey squeaked in terror. He dashed along the walls of the room, looking for his mousehole.

"It's a kitten!" cried Peggy, as Mickey squeezed through the hole.

"But it acts like a mouse," said Paul.

The children could not understand why the kitten had been so mouselike, but they decided to try to make friends with him.

That night, as Mickey came out of his hole, he nearly tripped over something lying right there in front of him. He sniffed at it. It was a dish, and in the dish was something to drink.

"What is it?" asked Mickey. Lester didn't know, but timidly tried a little. "No good," he said, shaking his whiskers.

Mickey tried it, tried some more, then some more and some more and more and more—until it was all gone.

"Mmmmm!" he said. "What wonderful stuff."

"It's probably poison and you'll get sick," said Lester disgustedly. But it wasn't poison and Mickey had a lovely feeling in his stomach from drinking it. It was milk, of course. And every night that week Mickey found a saucer of milk outside that same hole. He lapped up every drop.

"He drank it, he drank it!" cried Peggy and Paul happily each morning. They began to set out a saucerful in the daytime, too.

At first Mickey would drink the milk only when he was sure Peggy and Paul were nowhere around. Soon he grew bolder and began to trust them in the room with him.

And soon he began to let them come nearer and nearer and nearer still.

Then one day he found himself scooped up and held in Peggy's arms. He didn't feel scared. He felt fine. And he felt a queer noise rumble up his back and all through him. It was Mickey's first purr.

Peggy and Paul took Mickey to a shiny glass on the wall and held him close in front of it. Mickey, who had never seen a mirror, saw a cat staring at him there, a cat in Paul's hands, where he thought *he* was. He began to cry, and his cry, instead of being a squeak, was a mewing wail.

Finally Mickey began to understand that he was not a mouse like Lester and his sisters, but a cat like Hazel.

He stayed with Peggy and Paul that night, trying not to be afraid of his own cat-self. He still didn't quite believe it all, however, and next morning he crept back through his old hole straight to Mother Miggs.

"Am I really a cat?" he cried.

"Yes," said Mother Miggs sadly. And she told him the whole story of how he was adopted and brought up as a mouse. "We loved you and wanted you to love us," she explained. "It was the only safe and fair way to bring you up."

After talking with Mother Miggs, Mickey decided to be a cat in all ways. He now lives with Peggy and Paul, who also love him, and who can give him lots of good milk, and who aren't afraid of his purr or his meow.

Mickey can't really forget his upbringing, however. He takes an old rubber mouse of Peggy's to bed with him.

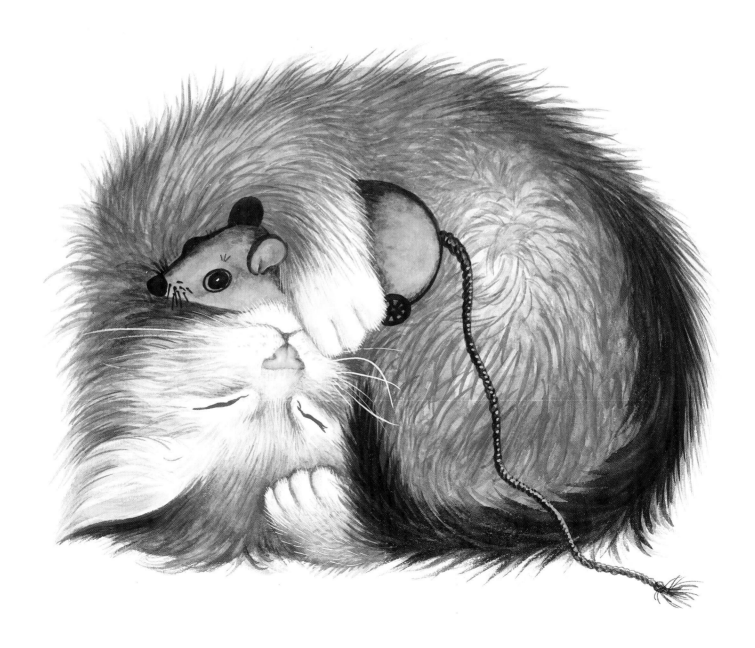

He often visits the Miggses in the indoor nest, where he nibbles cheese tidbits and squeaks about old times.

And of course he sees to it that Hazel no longer prowls in the pantry at night.

"Oh, I'm so fat and stuffed from eating so much in Hazel's pantry," Father Miggs often says happily to Mother Miggs. "I always said our Mickey would be a good thing for the family—and he is!"

Mister Dog

The Dog Who Belonged to Himself

written by Margaret Wise Brown

Once upon a time there was a funny dog named Crispin's Crispian. He was named Crispin's Crispian because he belonged to himself.

In the mornings, he woke himself up and he went to the icebox and gave himself some bread and milk. He was a funny old dog. He liked strawberries.

Then he took himself for a walk. And he went wherever he wanted to go.

But one morning he didn't know where he wanted to go.

"Just walk and sooner or later you'll get somewhere," he said to himself.

Soon he came to a place where there were lots of dogs. They barked at him and he barked back. Then they all played together.

But he still wanted to go somewhere, so he walked on until he came to a place where there were lots of cats and rabbits.

The cats and rabbits jumped in the air and ran. So Crispian jumped in the air and ran after them.

He didn't catch them because he ran bang into a little boy.

"Who are you and to whom do you belong?" asked the little boy.

"I am Crispin's Crispian and I belong to myself," said Crispian. "Who and what are you?"

"I am a boy," said the boy, "and I belong to myself."

"I am so glad," said Crispin's Crispian. "Come and live with me."

So the boy walked on with Crispian and threw him sticks to chase,

all through the shining, sun-drenched morning.

"I'm hungry," said Crispin's Crispian. "I'm hungry, too," said the little boy. So they went to a butcher shop—"to get his poor dog a bone," Crispian said.

Now, since Crispin's Crispian belonged to himself, he gave himself the bone and trotted home with it.

And the boy bought a big lamb chop and a bright green vegetable and trotted home with Crispin's Crispian.

Crispin's Crispian lived in a two-story doghouse in a garden.

And in his two-story doghouse he had a little fur living room with a warm fire that crackled all winter and went out in the summer.

His house was always warm. His house had a chimney for the smoke to go out.

And there was plenty of room in his house for the boy to live there with him.

Crispian went upstairs, and the boy went with him.

And upstairs Crispian had a little bedroom with a bed in it, and a place for his leash, and a pillow under which he hid his bones.

And he had windows to look out of and a garden to run around in any time he felt like running around in it. The garden was blooming with dogwood and dogtooth violets.

Crispian had a little kitchen upstairs in his two-story doghouse where he fixed himself a good meal three times a day because he liked to eat. He liked steaks and chops and roast beef and chopped meat and raw eggs.

This evening Crispian made a bone soup with lots of meat in it. He gave some to the boy, and the boy liked it. The boy didn't give Crispian his chop bone, but he did put some of his bright-green vegetable in the soup.

And what did Crispian do with his dinner?

Did he put it in his stomach?

Yes, indeed.

He chewed it up and swallowed it into his little fat stomach.

And what did the little boy do with his dinner?

Did he put it in his stomach?

Yes, indeed.

He chewed it up and swallowed it into his little fat stomach.

Crispin's Crispian was a *conservative*.
He liked everything at the right time—
    dinner at dinnertime,
    lunch at lunchtime,
    breakfast in time for breakfast,
    and sunrise at sunrise,
    and sunset at sunset.
    And at bedtime—
At bedtime he liked everything in its
own place—
    the cup in the saucer,
    the chair under the table,
    the stars in the heavens,
    the moon in the sky,
    and himself in his own little bed.

And then what did he do?

Then he curled in a warm little heap and went to sleep.
And he dreamed his own dreams.

That was what the dog who belonged to himself did.

And what did the boy who belonged to himself do?

The boy who belonged to himself curled in a warm little
heap and went to sleep. And he dreamed his own dreams.

That was what the boy who belonged to himself did.

GOOD NIGHT
AND
SWEET DREAMS.

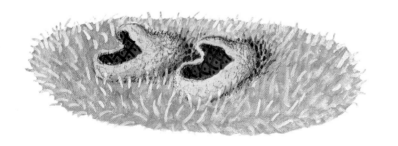